Tomorrow's Alphabet

By
George Shannon
Pictures by
Donald Crews

Greenwillow Books, New York

Watercolors were used for the full-color art. The text type is Akzidenz Grotesk.

Tomorrow's Alphabet
Text copyright © 1996
by George W. B. Shannon
Illustrations copyright © 1996
by Donald Crews

For information address
HarperCollins Children's
Books, an imprint of
HarperCollins Publishers,
10 East 53rd Street,
New York, NY 10022.

09 10 11 12 13 SCP 10 9 8

Manufactured in China
by South China Printing
Company Ltd.

www.harperchildrens.com

Library of Congress
Cataloging-in-Publication Data

Shannon, George.
Tomorrow's alphabet / by
George Shannon;
pictures by Donald Crews.
    p.   cm.
"Greenwillow Books."
1. English language—Alphabet—
Juvenile literature.
[1. Alphabet.]   I. Crews,
Donald, ill.   II. Title.
PE1155.S5   1996   [E]—dc20
94-19484   CIP   AC
ISBN 0-688-13504-8 (trade)
ISBN 0-688-13505-6 (lib. bdg.)
ISBN 0-688-16424-2 (pbk.)

For **B**rian, **A**ndrew, and
Kaitlyn **S**hannon
–G. S.

For **A**nn, **N**ina, and **A**my,
and the **G**ang at **G**reenwillow
and **S**usan and **A**va (who put her foot in it)
–D. C.

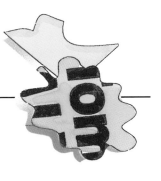

A is for seed–

tomorrow's

APPLE

B

is for eggs–

tomorrow's

BIRDS

c is for milk—

tomorrow's

CHEESE

D

is for
puppy–

tomorrow's

DOG

E is for campfire–

tomorrow's

EMBERS

F is for wheat–

tomorrow's

FLOUR

G is for bulbs–

tomorrow's

GARDEN

H

is for yarn–

tomorrow's

HAT

is for
water–

tomorrow's

ICE CUBES

J

**is for
pumpkin–**

tomorrow's

JACK-O'-LANTERN

K is for tomato—

L is for bud–

tomorrow's

LEAF

M

**is for
caterpillar–**

tomorrow's

MOTH

N

**is for
twigs–**

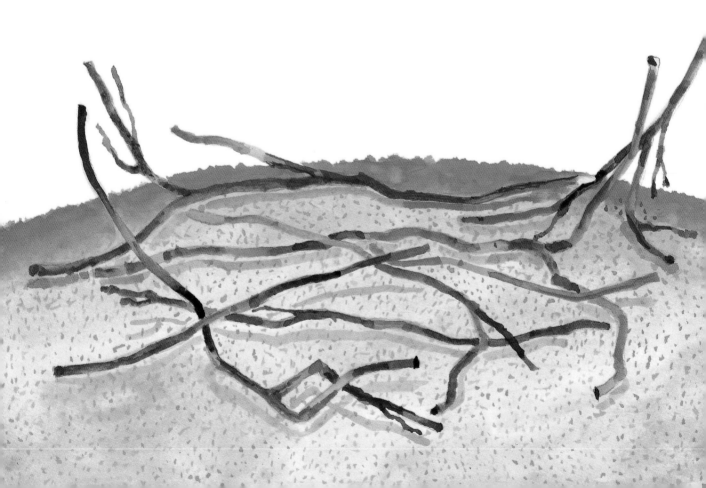

tomorrow's

NEST

O

is for acorn—

tomorrow's

OAK TREE

P **is for clay–**

tomorrow's

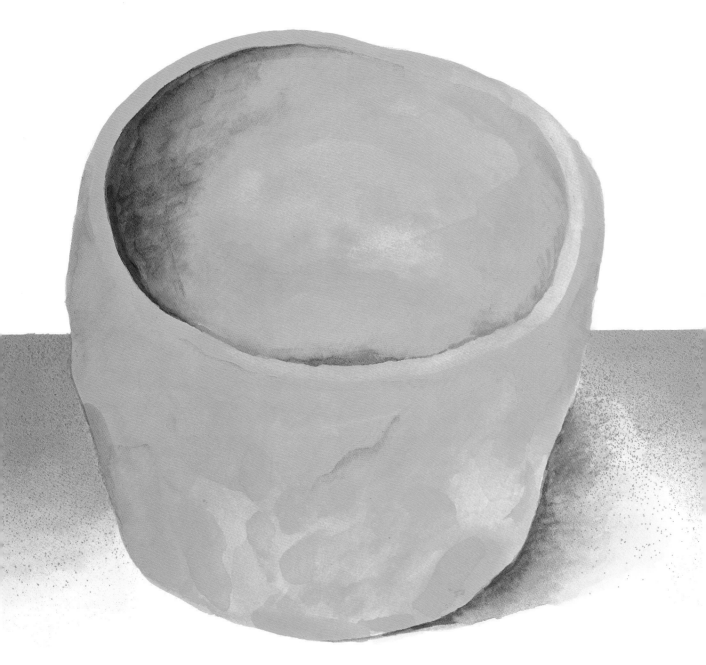

POT

Q is for scraps–

tomorrow's

QUILT

R  is for grapes–

tomorrow's

RAISINS

S

is for vegetables–

T is for bread–

tomorrow's

TOAST

U is for stranger–

tomorrow's

US

V is for paper–

tomorrow's

VALENTINE

W

is for stones–

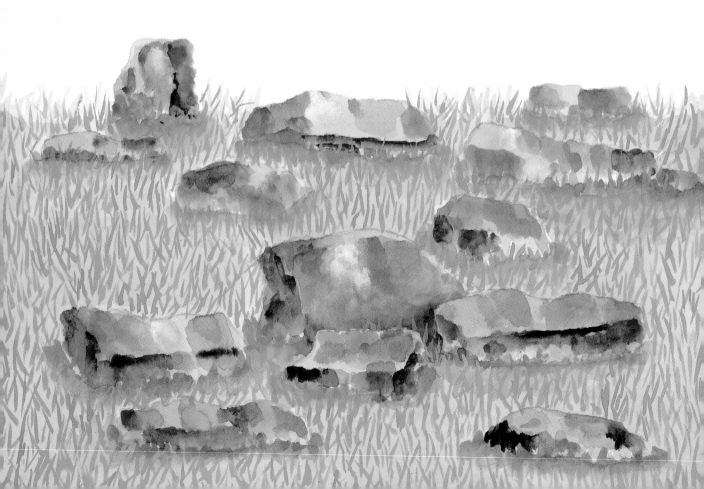

tomorrow's

WALL

X is for bones–

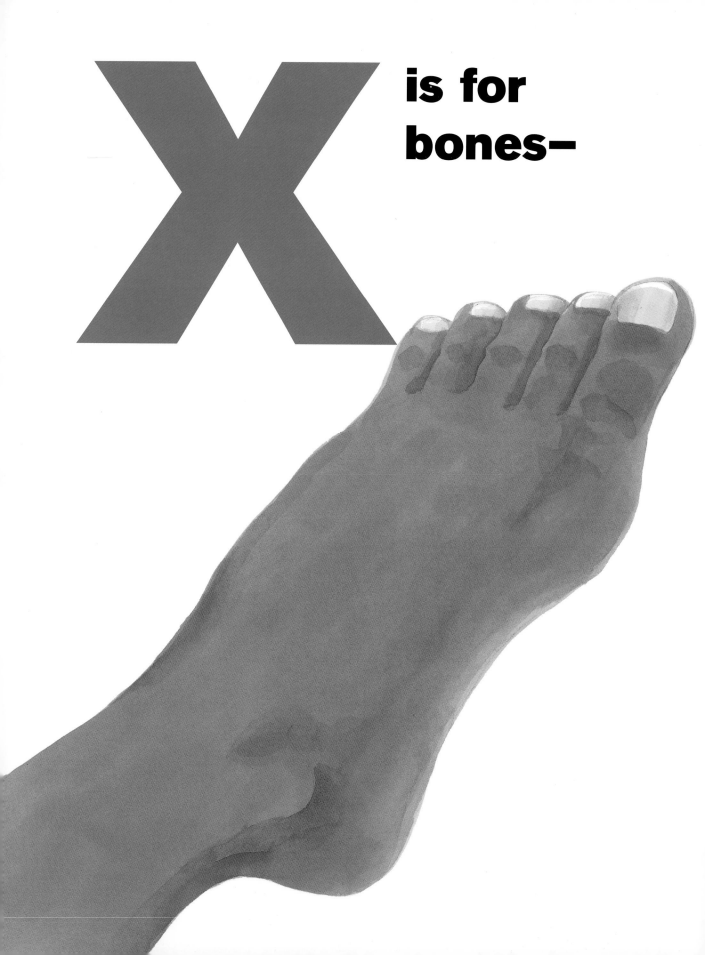

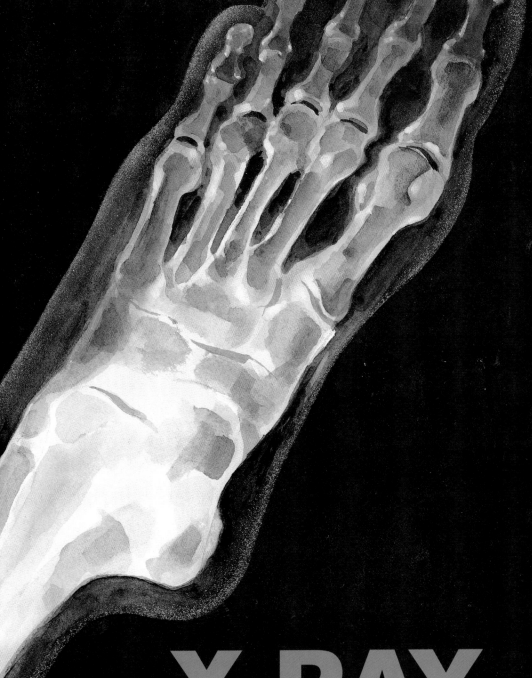

tomorrow's

X-RAY

Y is for sheep—

tomorrow's

100% WOOL

YARN

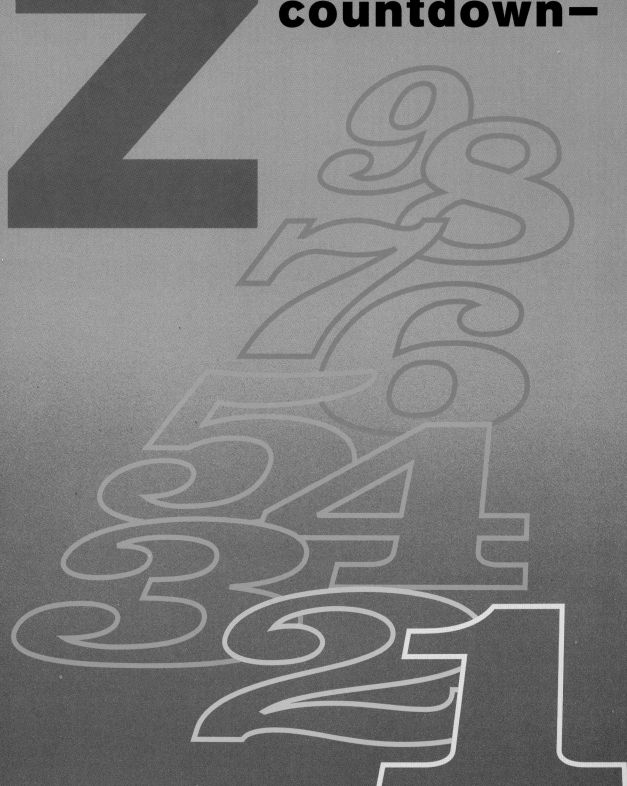

Z is for countdown—

tomorrow's

ZERO

ABCDE
FGHIJK
LMNOP
QRSTU
VWXYZ